Soldier's Son

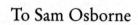

To Sam Osborne

Soldier's Son

Garry Kilworth

A & C Black • London

VICTORIAN FLASHBACKS

Soldier's Son • Garry Kilworth
A Slip in Time • Maggie Pearson
Out of the Shadow • Margaret Nash
The Voyage of the Silver Bream • Theresa Tomlinson

also available:

WORLD WAR II FLASHBACKS

The Right Moment • David Belbin
Final Victory • Herbie Brenn
Blitz Boys • Linda Newbery
Blood and Ice • Neil Tonge

First paperback edition 2002
First published 2001 in hardback by
A & C Black (Publishers) Ltd
37 Soho Square, London, W1D 3QZ

Text copyright © 2001 Garry Kilworth
Cover illustration copyright © 2001 Mike Adams

ISBN 0-7136-6079-1

A CIP catalogue record for this book is available
from the British Library.

Printed and bound in Great Britain by
Creative Print & Design (Wales), Ebbw Vale.

Contents

Contents

Author's Note

In the early 1850s Turkey had an empire of which Russia was quite jealous. Russia decided to attack Turkey and began by sinking its fleet of warships. Britain and France were worried about a big country like Russia becoming even more powerful, so they went to war to help Turkey fight the invaders.

In February 1854 the British army, which was called the 'Army of the East', set sail for Russia. First they landed at Constantinople, (which is now called Istanbul) the capital of Turkey. From there they went on into the Black Sea, stopping first at a small port called Varna, then on to the Crimean peninsula, which was part of Russia.

The British and the French armies landed in the Crimea and fought their first battle on the River Alma. The Russians lost this fight and retreated to a city called Sebastopol. The allied armies followed them and fought several more battles. The Battle of Balaclava, where the famous mistake called the Charge of the Light Brigade happened, and the Battle of Inkerman, were the two biggest of these battles. (See map on p.82.)

This was at a time when there were still muskets which had to be loaded by ramming the charge and the ball down the barrel of the weapon with a long metal rod. A British soldier could fire his musket three or four times in one minute. Cannons had to be hauled by horses or oxen over thick mud and were very difficult to manage. When the allies landed it was September and as the weather got colder, so did the men. Soon they were in a freezing Russian winter with only ragged tents and one single uniform each to keep them warm. Many of them died of the cold and disease. In fact in the whole war in which 20,000 British soldiers died only 4,000 were killed in battle. Some of these were boys of nine or ten years of age: cabin boys on ships or drummer boys in the army.

In those days too, some families were allowed to go with the British army when it went off to fight in foreign lands. These were called 'camp followers' and the wives of the soldiers often helped the regiment doctors to treat the sick and wounded.

In 1856 the allied armies stormed Sebastopol and captured it from the Russians and so the war was over. The Russian army retreated and the British and French soldiers were finally allowed to go home. Afterwards everyone agreed that it had been an unnecessary war - as most wars are - and that it should never have happened in the first place.

1 ◆ Off to War

The band was playing *Cheer, Boys, Cheer!* Tim Baker's father, a corporal in the 95th Foot Regiment, was looking tall and proud in his red coat and shako hat as he marched down the street in Portsmouth. Tim watched him go by and caught his eye. He saw his father wink. Then he was gone and the rest of the infantry battalion flowed past Tim and his mother.

It was Easter, 1854. Portsmouth's streets were full of holidaymakers. It seemed the whole of Britain was there, waving handkerchiefs at the soldiers. A local boy, standing behind Tim, said scornfully, 'They're out of step. They can't march properly. Wait till...' But he never finished his sentence because Tim rounded on him furiously. The boy was about his age, ten or eleven years old. Tim stepped forward.

'What do you know? That's the best regiment in England, that is. That's the Derbyshire regiment. What do you know, anyway?'

Startled, the other boy stepped back, bunching

his fists. But before it could come to anything, there came the clip-clop sound of horses' hooves on the cobbles. Both boys turned again, to watch the Hussars go by. Everything stopped for the Hussars, resplendent in their cherry-coloured trousers. Then came the cream of the infantry, the Guards, with their tall bearskin hats. They marched as if they were wooden puppets painted in bright colours. Tim would swear on his deathbed that his father's regiment was the best in the land, but oh, to be a guardsman!

When the parade was over, the crowd broke up. Tim's adversary had vanished into the Portsmouth alleys. Tim and his mother made their way back to the barracks near the dockside. Tomorrow they were to sail with Tim's father to go to war with Russia. Some wives were allowed to follow their husbands to battle. Tim's mother considered herself lucky to be chosen to go. And Tim would go with her.

'Why can't I join the regiment?' Tim grumbled, as they walked along. 'Why won't you let me, Ma? Sean O'Reilly is only ten years old. He's got a sword.' He paused to reflect, thinking of the long curved sabres of the Hussars. 'It's a short one, but it's a sword all right.'

Sean was one of Tim's friends. A boy from an Irish family, recruited when the regiment had been in Liverpool. Although they were the Derbyshire regiment, they picked up soldiers wherever they went. There were Scots and Welsh, not to mention south of England men. Some of the accents were hard for Tim's mother to understand, but Tim got used to them very quickly.

'Sean O'Reilly is Sean O'Reilly,' said Tim's mother, Kate, pulling her worn grey shawl over her shoulders.

Tim knew what that meant. Tim's mother was the daughter of an innkeeper and considered herself to be a cut above most of the other regiment wives and soldiers. It meant that Tim Baker was meant for higher things than the army could offer.

The billet where the family slept was a long room full of soldier's beds called 'cots' with only a few centimetres between each one. Some of them, the family cots, had blankets round them for screens. The room was crowded, thick with smoke. There was the damp smell of drying washing, which hung from the rafters and dripped on beds and people alike. Tim's mother went to her husband. He was sitting on his neighbour's cot smoking a clay pipe. He kissed his wife's cheek, then ruffled Tim's hair.

'What did you think of it, eh? Grand?'

Soldiers were taking off their rough tunics and draping them over any spare piece of furniture they could find. A sergeant was chewing on a smoked haddock. Jack Piggot, a fourteen-year-old bugler, signalled to Tim, who went across to his cot. Jack was Tim's best friend. Jack had bow legs from rickets, which made him shorter than the other boys in the band. Tim never made fun of his size and that helped to make the friendship a good one, despite their difference in ages.

'How did I look?' said Jack, grinning. 'Did you hear all those people cheering? Usually they hate us soldiers in their town, but now there's a war, they love us.'

'You looked smart,' Tim assured his friend. 'I saw your bugle glint like gold from way off. Way off. Then up you come, behind it, cheeks puffed like sails. It was grand.'

Jack looked pleased. 'Did you really? Up I comes, behind it, eh? You have a way with words, Tim. Sergeant?' yelled Jack to his N.C.O., 'can I go down to the port, to see the boat?'

'Away you go, lad,' replied the sergeant, gruffly.

'Come on,' said Jack, putting on a small forage cap with the number 95 on the front. 'Let's go and see our boat. You coming, O'Reilly?'

'I'm with you,' replied the drummer boy.

The three boys left the barracks and walked through the Portsmouth streets, heading for the docks. Tim felt out of place with the other two, who still looked splendid in their uniforms. He wished, as he had wished a thousand times before, that he was in the regiment proper, and not just a camp follower, trotting on behind it with his mother. Oh, yes, they let him do chores, like making the cooking fires, and blacking boots, and pipe-claying the uniform straps. But it wasn't the same. It wasn't the same as walking through Portsmouth with people gawking and pointing, because you wore a red coat and smart trousers and a neat cap.

'Will you swap coats with me, Sean?' pleaded Tim. 'And can I wear the forage cap too?'

'All right,' said the accommodating Irish boy. 'Just for a while, mind.'

Tim eagerly put on the other boy's coat and hat. Then he marched beside Jack, saluting all the gentlemen and ladies who passed them. When a Hussar officer came along, Tim got flustered and went and saluted with the wrong hand. The officer stopped them, spoke to Sean severely for letting a civilian wear his red coat, then went on his way.

When he was out of sight the boys hooted in his direction.

'Ha! Cherry bum! Cherry bum!' yelled Tim, safe in the knowledge that the Hussar could not hear him.

The docks were alive with workers, loading stores onto ships, unloading cargo onto the dock. The three boys fought their way through the mass of bodies and finally stood on the quayside looking up at a tall, masted vessel.

'There she is,' said Jack. 'The *Empress*. That's our boat, lads. Don't she look something?'

A sailor, within earshot, said, 'She's a ship, lad. Never call her a boat, or you'll have my boot up your backside.'

'Ship,' murmured Tim, looking round at all the other vessels, dozens of them all at anchor or berthed at the quay. 'Look at that dark forest of masts. You could get lost in there. You could be left to starve and die, and never be found in a year of Sundays.'

Sean grinned and said, 'A way with words, our Tim.'

Tim's heart was beating fast. Tomorrow he was going on a ship. To foreign lands. To war against a foreign foe. This was the most exciting thing he had ever done in his life. He couldn't wait to hear the cannons blasting, the muskets cracking, the drums and fifes, the thunder of horses' hooves as the dashing cavalry went charging into the enemy, their swords flashing in the sunlight. He couldn't wait.

2 ◈ Sailing to Russia

Next day they were in the Bay of Biscay, on their way to the Mediterranean Sea. The ship was tossed about on giant waves like a toy. Tim spent his time in a crowded hold. He was sick, over and over again. The smell down there was awful, but he hardly noticed it, he was so ill. Once O'Reilly came to drag him up on deck, it was a bit better. There was a cold wind which bit into his lungs, and the salt spray in the air, to keep his mind off his stomach.

'Don't get under my feet, lads,' said a mariner, who barged through them. 'Find a place out of the way.'

Above the boys' heads sailors were like busy squirrels in the rigging, altering this, changing that, letting out sail, taking in sail. From time to time someone would yell an order from the quarterdeck and the business would increase in a flurry of running mariners.

'I'm glad I'm not a sailor,' said Sean, looking up to the dizzy heights in the rigging. 'I'd fall from there, for sure.'

By the time they reached the Mediterranean the sea was calm. They passed the Rock of Gibraltar and sailed on to a place called Constantinople, the capital of Turkey. Here the excitement increased. There were markets full of brass and glass, and wondrous carvings from Africa, and colours and smells to make Tim's head spin.

'I used to think Ilkeston market was exciting,' Tim told Sean, 'but when you come to places like this...'

Here was a spice market that covered ten acres of ground. Then another two acres of fabrics. Then gold, and silver and ivory. Not to mention exotic vegetables, meat and fish. Dark-skinned, olive-skinned, light-skinned people thronged the streets. Here were children more ragged and poorer even than Tim had ever been. Here were children who fought over a crust of bread and ate cabbage stalks from the gutter. It was certainly a place which made Tim bless his father's pay - three pence a day after stoppages.

From Constantinople they sailed up the Black Sea coast, to a much smaller town called Varna. This was a very gentle landscape, with fruit bushes, trees, and warm sunshine. Here there were farms and people who were rough but still kind-hearted. Here life was easy for a while.

'This is better than back in Ilkeston,' said Tim, his head resting on a hillock. 'I could stay here for ever.'

'If you like,' replied Jack, 'but I want to get to the war in the Crimea. Them Russkis are sayin' they can beat us. Can you imagine, beating the British Army? Some hope they have, I can tell you.'

'Look,' Sean said, pointing, 'there's some Frenchies. Zouaves, they are. I can tell by their uniforms.'

Some blue-coated soldiers went by and called to the boys in French, laughing when Tim and his friends did not understand.

'We used to fight the Frenchies,' murmured Jack, 'but now they're our friends and allies.'

'Let's pretend we're still fighting them,' said Jack, 'since we haven't got any Russians to shoot at. Look, there's a ditch over there, with some good mud going to waste.'

The boys made some mud bombs and sat behind a hedge and waited. Pretty soon some French cavalry rode by.

'Now!' yelled Sean.

Up they popped from behind the hedge, all three boys. They lobbed their mud grenades and saw them splatter on the French uniforms.

'*Mon Dieu*!' came the cry, as a French hat went flying.

A second rider was hit full on the pelisse.

The horses skipped and danced. There was confusion amongst the French squadron. One trooper came charging towards the hedge, clearly intending to ride the boys down. He received a mud bomb full on the chest and was almost toppled from his saddle.

'A hit, a double hit!' cried Tim. 'Whey! They're coming after us. Run! Run!'

The boys scurried into a nearby apple orchard, knowing the horsemen would have difficulty following them into the trees. Sean and Jack had had the good sense to turn their jackets inside out and remove the number 95 from their forage caps. If they were caught at these pranks, they would be severely punished. Getting away with it though, they scrumped cherries from the trees, and laughing, played hide-and-seek in the tall grass beyond.

'This is like being on the farm at home,' said Jack, lying on his back under the sun and chewing a straw, 'except we don't have to work from dawn till dusk.'

The pleasant life at Varna did not last long. A dreaded disease called cholera crept into the camps and before long men were dying one after another. Tim was taken to a barn on the edge of the town to be out of the way of the disease, as two regiment wives had died already. There was no way to bury the dead in the hard ground, so weights were tied to the corpses and they were thrown into the sea. But some didn't sink, and bobbed around like ghastly phantoms in the water.

Tim had seen death in England. People froze or starved there, too. But the bodies were usually taken away and buried very quickly. Here he saw men stagger along with horrible yellow complexions, fall from the marching columns on parade, to be dragged away by bandsmen. Death was everywhere. Horses too, were dropping and dying in the heat, and this seemed to upset the soldiers more than anything else.

'Oh, hurry up and let's get to the war,' Tim prayed at night by his bed of straw. 'Let's shoot them Russkis, win the battle, and go home.'

It wasn't until the autumn that they went on board the ships again, setting off over the Black Sea for the Crimea itself. They landed in a grey-looking bay called Calamita. When Tim and his mother went ashore, after the battalions had disembarked, they expected to find the tents already up. But all they found were men trying to camp out in the mud on open ground. It was drizzling, there were few trees under which to shelter, and the first night was spent soaking wet, cold and hungry. There was no wood for fires, the tents had been forgotten, and the soldiers had only the uniforms they stood up in.

'Let's get to that battle,' growled Tim to anyone who would listen. 'We can beat the Russians, I know it.'

It was all he could think of during the next four days, to get into the fight. Jack was the same. And Sean. They wanted the trumpets blaring, the drums drumming and the cannons roaring. It was to be glorious. Everyone said so. Once the battle was over and the bodies cleared away, the world would be a nice, tidy place, full of heroes. Not full of that disease which made men into trembling wrecks.

And it wasn't only cholera. Now there was a host of other illnesses, one or two of which kept making Tim dash away behind rock or bush, with, 'I won't be a minute, Ma!' and spending half an hour crouched and cold with the cramps in his abdomen. In this camp there were no vegetables to eat and all Tim was given was salted meat and biscuit. Even water was hard to find at times. It wasn't how he imagined. Everyone had said what a wonderful war it would be, but Tim was quickly losing patience. When would the fighting come?

'It'll come soon enough,' said Corporal Baker to his angry eleven-year-old son. 'And then we'll wish ourselves pedlars, clerks or farmhands again.'

Lord Raglan, the Commander-in-Chief, rode by one grey morning. Tim wanted to ask him when the fighting would start, but he was afraid of this one-armed man on a tall horse. There were officers all around him and anyway, Tim knew he was not allowed to speak to a general. His father would be in trouble if he did. So Tim just had to try to make fires with twisted grass, which never worked properly, and hope that perhaps the next day the army would march into battle against the foe.

3 ❖ Into Battle

After a week of waiting, the day finally came! It was a bright day in September, 1854.

The whole army, all thirty thousand of them including the French and the Turks, were spread out as far as the eye could see. There were the British redcoats, the blue French Zouaves and the Turkish Bashi-Bazouks in their bright pantaloons, waistcoats and floppy hats. Such a blaze of colour. Bronze cannons and howitzers gleamed in the sunlight. Horses looked groomed and sleek. Jack and Sean were in their places in the line nearby, looking as proud as punch. How Tim envied them, but it would all be soon over, and even if Tim joined the army tomorrow, he would not get to fight in a glorious battle.

'Good luck, Jack. Good luck, Sean,' he called. 'See you after the fighting. You'll be heroes, you will.'

Tim's mother grabbed his hand and gripped it rather hard. He looked up to see her face was white.

'Why, what's the matter, Ma?'

'Men will die today,' she said, 'and there'll be widows grieving when darkness falls.'

But Tim thought she was being too dramatic. After all, it would be mostly Russians who would be killed. Only one or two British soldiers, surely.

Then the army started to march, trumpets blaring, drums rat-tat-tatting, French bugles tooting. This was more like it! It was just how Tim had imagined. The women and children followed on behind the lines of red and blue. The marching column that was over two miles in width scattered wildlife before it. Weasels, stoats, rabbits, quail, hares, mice, voles: all were herded before the pounding of thirty thousand pairs of boots.

Not far away, on the heights above a river called the Alma, thirty-three thousand Russian soldiers waited to do battle with the oncoming foe. They had built a platform just behind the battle lines for the civilians from Sebastopol city, who sat there as if watching a play: gentlemen in smart suits, ladies in silk dresses spinning parasols in their white-gloved hands.

Tim and the other camp followers found themselves a good view from a ridge to the left of the battle. They could look down at the fighting from a safe distance.

The battle began around noon. First a single Russian cannon sent a black ball of iron flying through the air towards the redcoats. They saw it coming and they laughed, parting ranks, so that it bounced between them. But more cannons began firing, then rockets and shells began bursting over the heads of the soldiers, sending hot shards of metal into their ranks. The sounds were deafening. Dark, stinking smoke began to gather and drift over the landscape as the Russians set fire to farm buildings in an attempt to block the enemies' advance. Soon it was difficult for Tim to see what was going on.

For a while all was quiet on the ridge as the followers watched fearfully, but then when men began falling in a hail of lead bullets, one of the women shrieked, 'We have to go and help.'

Tim's mother told him, 'You stay here, mind!' Then she followed the other wives streaming down the hillside to the baggage train at the back of the battle. Tim could still pick her out as she started to help the wounded men being brought out of the fighting by the bandsmen. He could see the regimental surgeons here and there, cutting, chopping, bandaging wounds. There was no way Tim could stay on the ridge. He ran down to join them, only to have a soldier blunder out of the smoke, almost on top of him. Tim was nearly sick when he saw that the man was carrying his own severed arm.

'Tim, help him,' cried a pale-faced Jack, suddenly amongst them. He had another man weighing him down, bending his bow legs even further. 'This one's...' he let him fall. 'This one's dead, I think.'

But the soldier with the arm had gone, walking resolutely back towards the baggage train. His movements had been mechanical. It seemed he hardly knew what he was doing or where he was.

'Are we winning the battle, Jack?' asked Tim, feeling much younger than his fourteen-year-old friend.

Jack gave him a sickly grin. 'Who knows, Tim? There are men with shattered bodies out there who need me. There are men with broken heads. I must go...'

And gone he was, back into the smoke of war.

Before Tim could gather his wits, a cannonball landed right by him, sending up a spray of earth which covered his head and shoulders. It ploughed on into a wagon not far away. The horses bolted. Aghast, Tim stared at the round dent in the turf where the shot had first landed and shattered some rock beneath.

He heard a voice close at hand. 'Water!' croaked a soldier, lying on the ground nearby. 'Get me some water, boy.'

Tim shook himself and ran back to the wagons to find one of the personal kettles that British soldiers carried as part of their kit. He filled it full of water from a barrel then hurried back to the soldier, who was now sitting up.

'Here's some water, sir.'

'Thank you, boy.'

The redcoat drank heavily. There was blood on the collar of his uniform, trickling down from his ear. Tim left the man to go to a Frenchman, whose leg twisted at a funny angle from his body. The Frenchman cried, '*De l'eau, mon ami!*'

'What's that?' said Tim. 'I don't understand.'

'He'll want the water too,' said the British soldier. 'Here now, give him some of this.' He held out the camp kettle.

So it went. The smoke became thicker. Fresh men were sent up to the front line, more wounded men came back. Those who did not come back were either heroes or they were dead.

Up on the ridge above the Alma the fiercest of fights was in progress. After some time the grey-coated Russians began to retreat. The ladies and gentlemen on the platform dropped their purses, their parasols, their hats, and began running back to Sebastopol.

Down with the wounded, Tim raced around doing what he could, but still the noise from the guns was ear-splitting. Still the shells came hurtling down to explode nearby. Not once did he stop to think about the horror all around him.

4 ❖ The Aftermath

After the battle, which ended in the late afternoon, and for the whole night following, wounded men lay out amongst the dead on the battlefield, crying for water. Only when the dawn came was there a chance to get to them. A strange sight met the rescuers as they ventured out onto the battlefield in the early morning light. The landscape was littered with soldier's shako hats and kettles, thousands of them, all wet with morning dew and glinting in the sunlight.

'They got in the way,' explained a soldier who'd survived, just as amazed by the sight of the kettles and hats as Tim was. 'We had to drop them on the way into the firing. They got in the way.'

On the French half of the field it was haversacks. Thousands of those had been deliberately left behind when the French infantry went into fight. Now, however, the Zouaves were going back to collect them, because their blankets and spare clothes were in those packs.

Tim's father survived the battle. He smiled at Tim

but he looked exhausted. Now Tim went searching for his two friends, Sean and Jack. He found Sean asleep under a wagon, damp with the dew, and he woke him.

'Sean, are you all right?'

Sean opened his eyes blearily, looked startled for a minute, then sat up and rubbed his face.

'Yes,' he said. 'But I wish I was back in County Cork where I was born. It was bad, Tim. It was very bad. I don't know how many men got hurt.'

Tim said, 'I heard tell 2000 casualties on our side.'

'And the Russkis?'

'Thousands more.'

Sean took a drink of water from his kettle. Then he turned to face Tim. 'I never thought I'd say this,' he said, 'but I feel sorry for those Russian soldiers today, Tim. They fought hard. But we had better rifles than them. They had old, worn-out things. If it weren't for that, why, it would've been worse.'

'But our men were brave.'

'Oh, they were brave all right.' Sean grabbed Tim's coat collar and pulled his face close to his own. Tim could see Sean's eyes were red with crying. He had probably been crying in his sleep. He looked haggard but he still looked like a lost young child. 'It's my eleventh birthday today, Tim.

On that battlefield yesterday, playing my drum, helping the wounded men - why, I thought I would die before my birthday. It's not much, is it, to be just ten years old - to die like that. There were boys out there...'

Tim, shaking himself because he too was raw from the terrible effects of seeing men die for the first time, seeing men shattered and broken by cannonballs and shells, prised Sean's fingers from his collar.

'Yes, yes - I know. I saw it too, from far back it's true, but I saw some things. Where's Jack?'

A deep, dark light came into Sean's eyes. He looked over his shoulder towards the encampment. Behind the boys, soldiers were beginning to rise from the ground where they had slept with just a single blanket. Fires were being lit. A shot rang out as someone killed a hare or quail for breakfast.

Others were gathering grapes in a deserted vineyard that had been blasted by round shot. Further off, women, bent and cowled with shawls, were searching amongst the dead bodies for their husbands and all too often a horrible wail of distress rent the morning air.

Sean whispered, 'He's gone, Tim. Run away. He was here with me under the wagon and he said he had to go.'

'Deserted?' Tim's mind reeled. His friend, a coward?

'Gone, up into the hills.'

'Not Jack? Why did he go?'

'He had to stick his sword in a Russki, Tim. To save me.' Tears came to Sean's eyes again and he wiped them away with his dirty sleeve, his face once more full of fear. 'This Russki was going to run me through with his bayonet and Jack stabbed him in the side. We saw the Russki fall over, grabbing at Jack's sword, trying to pull it out. Then we left him, yelling at us in that funny way they have. And then he fell to the ground and died. Jack was sick. In the middle of the night he woke me up and said he was running away.'

Tim's voice was tight. 'He shouldn't have gone.' Something in the way Tim said the words made Sean's face harden. 'Jack's not a coward, Tim.'

'Seems like he is.'

'You never had to kill anyone.' Sean looked into the middle distance, suddenly becoming very old in Tim's eyes. 'It wasn't a good thing at all. Not at all. A soldier's job is to kill people in war, but when you come to do it – well, I'm glad it wasn't me. Jack did it because he had to, to save me. But it was bad. I could see from his face afterwards. It was very bad.'

He turned to face Tim again. 'He didn't run away because he's scared of dying in battle. He ran because he doesn't want to kill again.'

'When they catch him,' said Tim, 'they'll hang him for sure.'

Sean didn't say anything in answer to this. Instead, he went to forage for scraps of wood to make a fire. Sean was always making tea for the soldiers of the regiment. They had come to expect it from him.

Tim went back to his mother and father. For an hour or two he simply sat there, thinking about things. Tim's mother, Kate, went off again to assist with the sick and wounded. They had to be helped down to the ships, so that they could be taken back to the hospital in Turkey. There were no ambulance wagons. Only the French had those. A lot of the sick and injured would die on the voyage, since no doctors could be spared to go with them.

Tim pipe-clayed his father's white straps and at the end of it he came to a decision. He was going to make up a white lie, to protect his friend from capture.

'Dad, you know Jack Piggot? They say he was taken prisoner by the Russkis.'

Tim's father blew smoke into the air. 'Who says?'

'I was speaking to some men from the Guards – the Coldstream Guards – one of them knew Jack and said he was taken.'

'Poor lad. I hope they remember that he's only a child.'

Tim had sown the seeds. Now, with Sean's help, he began spreading the rumour that Jack had been captured by the Russians. In that way there would be no search for him as a deserter. Tim wondered where Jack had really gone. Perhaps he was just hiding in some cave, or wood? Cold, afraid, and hungry?

5 ◈ The Deserter

But Jack hadn't fared so badly. He'd spent the night in an orchard to the north of the battle. The next morning, just when Tim had been hearing of his desertion, Jack was eating a ripe pear for his breakfast. But there was no water. Jack decided to risk heading for a farmhouse he could see in the distance. Once there he drank from a cattle trough in a field at the back of the farm. Then he sat down beside the trough and tried to marshal his thoughts.

'What am I to do? I'm a deserter now. They'll hang me for sure. You can't run away in the middle of a war and not be hanged.'

But the thought of being executed for cowardice and desertion in the face of the enemy was not as terrible as the memory of war itself. In one day, Jack had seen arms and legs blown off men standing just a metre away from him. He had been splattered with the blood of others. He knew he could not face that again. Jack was a farm labourer's son, from Norfolk, and up until now the only creatures he had seen slaughtered in such a way were livestock. He didn't blame the Russian soldiers. Some of them were boys like him. They were just doing what they were told to do by their officers.

'What are ye doing here, laddie?'

The language was English but the accent was Scottish. A man's shadow fell over him. Jack jumped to his feet that instant, thinking he had been caught. Already? It seemed so unfair.

The man before him was wearing brown tweeds and a collarless shirt. His face looked lean and hard. Jack noticed he had big hands, ingrained with soil. But he didn't seem angry at all. Just very dour.

Jack knew he was wearing his red coat. So though his hat had gone there was no doubting he was a soldier.

'Are ye looking to thieve from my farm, son? Ye'll get nothing here.'

'I - I wasn't stealing. I've run away.'

The man's blue eyes changed from steel blue to a softer hue.

'Run away, is it? That's a serious business for a soldier. How old are ye, laddie?'

'Fourteen, sir.'

'Almost a man, eh?'

Jack could not tell whether he was being made fun of or not. The farmer was a very serious-looking person.

'Is this your farm, sir?'

'It is indeed. We're not all Tartars and Cossacks, ye understand. There's more than one farm owned by a Scot or an Englishman in the Crimean peninsula. But this one's mine and very proud I am of it.'

Jack remembered that on the flank march south to the battle they had passed a large farm belonging to a Mr Mackenzie.

'You should be proud,' replied Jack. 'It looks a good one.'

'Oh, ye know about these things, do ye?'

'I'm a farm worker's boy myself, sir. I was raised running around a farm in Norfolk. I know a good one, when I see it. Listen, sir, you wouldn't need any help I suppose? I'm a good worker. I can do most jobs around the farm – any jobs, that is. I'd work for no pay. Just my keep.'

The farmer took a step back. His eyes narrowed.

'Oh, I don't know about that. Harbouring a deserter?'

'You could give me some different clothes. I'd be glad to burn these,' he looked down at himself. 'I would indeed, sir. You wouldn't regret it. If I'm caught, I'll tell them I got the clothes from somewhere else and that I told you I was a camp follower, not a soldier. You can hire who you please. There are travellers with the army who are not even family. Just ordinary people looking for excitement.'

'Ye'll be referring to the *travelling gentlemen*? But you're no gentleman, laddie. Anyone with half-an-eye can see that. Travelling gentlemen buy their passage to the Crimea. You obviously haven't a penny to your name.'

'Please, mister. Please think about it. If you say no, then I'll walk away and not bother you again. Do you have a wife, sir? Do you wish to ask your wife if I should stay?'

'Yes, I have a wife, but she's a local woman. A Tartar. And if I know her well, which I do, I know she's got a heart as soft as a plum pudding.' The Scot stared hard at Jack for a full five minutes, before saying, 'It's true I could do with some help around here. Ye look a strong enough lad. A farming boy, ye say? Well, let's give it a try. The British Army has no hold on me, here. I'm a civilian. What's the matter with yer legs? Rickets, is it?'

'Yes.'

'A farm labourer's son with rickets? That's usually a townie's disease.'

'I was very ill when I was little. But I'm strong enough now. Strong as a horse.'

The farmer motioned for Jack to follow him back to the house. There Jack met Mrs Robertson, who spoke no English at all, but had expressive eyes which sympathised with Jack's plight. Mr Robertson told his wife everything and true to her nature she said that they should help the boy, but first she wanted to know the answer to a question. She asked it through her husband who translated for her.

'My wife wants to know what you've done wrong. Have ye murdered an officer?'

'No - no, sir. Not that. Not ever. No. I found I can't kill, ma'am. I can't do it. I'm a bugler. I love to make music, but I'm expected to kill people too, and I can't do it.' He put out his trembling hands and tears came to his eyes. 'Yesterday I had to kill a man. A Russki man. He had done nothing to me, but he was going to stab my friend. I - I watched him die. He bled to death before my eyes.'

When the farmer translated this speech for his wife, her eyes softened again. She spoke to her husband in a tongue that sounded strange to Jack's ears.

'My wife says ye can stay,' said the Scot. 'Ye ken,

of course, that ye can never go home now? They'll post yer name up in the parish church, as a coward and a deserter, and as soon as ye poke yer nose back there, ye'll be turned over to the authorities?'

'Rather that than kill another man.'

6 ✥ The Charge of the Light Brigade

Tim and Sean were on the move again. The French and British armies, and their Turkish allies, moved south to lay siege to Sebastopol. Sebastopol was a large port, a city, on the Black Sea. It was guarded on the sea side by forts. The strongest of these was the Star Fort, which had cannons that could destroy British and French naval vessels should they go too close.

On the land side the Russians dug in, swiftly building fortifications and digging trenches. There was already a very large Russian army inside the walls of Sebastopol, and it was being strengthened by the day. Soon they would outnumber the invaders.

The French built a small town to the south of Sebastopol. They had wooden huts and canteens and a hospital. But the British were badly organised and badly supplied. They lived in tents which were so old they were rotting on their poles. They had only the clothes they stood up in, with just a spare shirt and spare socks, if they were lucky. Uniforms which had been red when they started out almost a year ago, had faded to purple. Every man was filthy. Disease was still rife. Life was miserable for the soldiers who had to dig trenches then live in them day and night.

Lord Raglan ordered that British guns should blast away at Sebastopol night and day until the Russians surrendered.

Tim's father went up to live in the trenches at the front. Tim and his mother stayed in a hovel on the edge of Balaclava harbour, where the British ships were moored. Life was hard for them too, with little food, and muddy, dirty conditions. Tim often wondered what had become of Jack and whether he was still alive.

One morning one of the wives came running into the hovel where Tim and his mother were trying to wash clothes. She looked distraught and angry.

'They're coming!' cried the woman. 'The Russians. The Turks have run away. It's all up with us.'

Tim rushed outside. True enough, there were Turkish soldiers racing towards the harbour, shouting, 'Boat! Boat!'

A British naval officer came striding down the muddy track.

'What's happening?' asked Kate. 'Have we been overrun?'

The officer paused and said, 'No, no. It's the guns, the cannons in the redoubts on the hills. They've been captured by the Russians. The Turkish gunners fought hard, but they had to retreat in the end. There were too many of the enemy. You can't blame them.'

'What shall we do?'

'Do? Stay here, ma'am. Stay here. The 93rd Sutherland Highlanders are guarding the pass. They'll stop any Russian attack on the harbour, you can be sure of that.'

With these words he was gone, towards one of the ships.

Without another word to his mother, Tim raced off. If there was to be a battle he wanted to see it. He made his way up the track until he reached the battleground. There he climbed a hill. He was just in time to see the Cossacks charge the Highlanders. The thin red line of Highlanders, wearing kilts and bonnets, fired into the mass of Russian cavalry. Several riders fell from their saddles. The Russian squadrons still kept coming. The Highlanders fired again. Still more men fell from their horses. A final volley and the Russians veered away, riding back up into the hills from whence they had come.

But there were many more of them! Tim could see that. There was a huge mass of Russian cavalry in the next valley. More sightseers climbed the hill on which he was standing. One of them spoke. A well-dressed, bearded man, rather large, with a notebook in his hand.

'Look! There's our Heavy Brigade.'

Tim stared. True enough the British Heavy Brigade of cavalry was riding down the valley below.

'They're charging!' cried Tim. 'They're charging the Russian cavalry.'

The Heavy Brigade of dragoons - big men on big horses with big swords - crashed into the Russian horsemen. They flailed around with their weapons, but the greatcoats of both armies were so thick the blades of the swords often bounced off them. Still the Heavy Brigade routed the Russian cavalry, sending them back into the hills. It was an exciting engagement, from a distance, and it had Tim wishing he were a trooper down there, swishing his sword through the air, riding to triumph and victory.

Not long afterwards, he changed his mind. Because what he saw next was the Light Brigade –

lightly armed men on fast horses – charging the Russian cannons and being blasted to pieces. It *had* to be a mistake! What could have caused that doomed charge? The Hussars and Lancers in their beautiful uniforms, on their wonderful light horses, were cut to ribbons by grapeshot and canister. The Russians had loaded their cannons with small pieces of metal and musket balls, and sent out a hail of shot which ripped men from their horses, and killed their mounts. The Light Brigade did not stand a chance. They rode down the valley that was lined with Russian riflemen, into the hot, spitting mouths of the big guns. At the end of the charge the survivors had to ride all the way back again, again through a storm of hot metal and bullets. Not many returned. Not many at all.

The pride of the British Army had been destroyed.

Tim was pale and shaking. He couldn't believe what he had seen. A few bedraggled riders made it back to the British line. Others walked back, their horses having been killed. Most lay dead or seriously wounded out in the valley, beyond the reach of the bandsmen whose job it was to carry the injured back to the surgeons. It was an ugly sight.

When, a little later, the infantry came up, the

Russians began to retreat once more. The Battle of Balaclava, unlike the Battle of the Alma, had been neither won nor lost.

The war became a way of life for Tim and his parents in their separate places as once more there was stalemate. The big guns pounded away at each other, from Sebastopol into the trenches, and from the siege line into Sebastopol. There were skirmishes and little forays, there were sharpshooters to contend with, there were comings and goings of small bands. Autumn was slipping away. Soon the allied army would be in the throes of a Russian winter and all they had to protect them were torn and tattered tents.

7 ❖ The Letter

With wagons and horses going back and forth, with men marching here and there, the ground at Balaclava was churned into a swamp. There was mud everywhere. Tim spent hours struggling through the mire, trying to find wood for a fire, or going on some errand. There was a small hospital just outside Balaclava – simply a house which had been taken over and called a hospital en rule and Kate often helped to nurse the soldiers there. There wasn't much anyone could do for them. Medicines were few and far between and no one really knew how to treat cholera, dysentery or wounds that had turned to gangrene.

Men such as Lord Cardigan, who had led the disastrous charge of the Light Brigade, lived aboard their yachts. They were relatively warm and safe.

But it was a miserable time for the soldiers. Spare clothes still had not arrived for the men in the battlefield trenches, or if they had they rotted on the quays. No one was allowed to open any crates or bales that did not have the proper certificate from

London. These certificates never seemed to arrive. Meanwhile, surgeons worked by candlelight because stocks of lamp oil could not be released from the store houses on the wharves.

One night, Tim was standing by a French camp fire, trying to get warm when he felt a tug on his sleeve.

'Psst. Tim. It's me.'

Alarmed, he turned, to see Jack crouched in the darkness, trying not to be seen by anyone.

Tim slipped back to join his friend. Jack must have thought it safe enough to come near the French camp, where no one would recognise him. He drew Tim even further into the darkness, behind some French huts, where they would not be overheard.

'Jack.'

'Tim,' said Jack, smiling. 'It's good to see you.'

'You ran away,' blurted Tim accusingly. 'You ran off.'

Jack stood there, silently, looking into Tim's eyes. 'I know,' he said at last. 'But I've done it, and that's that. I've got work on a farm now, I can't look back. I'm sorry if you feel ashamed of me.'

Tim looked down at his feet. 'I - I don't blame you, Jack. I'm all mixed up. You didn't even say goodbye to me. War isn't what it's supposed to be, is it?'

Jack said bitterly, 'They told us it would be glorious. Well, it's not. War is people being blown to bits. War is being freezing cold. War is being wet all the time and never getting dry.'

'I know,' said Tim, miserably. 'Some of the soldiers on the line – they're dying just from the cold and wet. They've got no proper clothes. No proper shelter. No fires to keep them warm. My dad...' He couldn't finish the sentence because he became choked inside.

'Is your father still all right?'

Tim nodded. 'He hasn't been shot and he hasn't got the cholera, but he's so thin now you wouldn't know him, Jack. You can't see his face for his beard, but the bones stick out all over him. We only get to see him once in a while.'

Jack said, 'You're not looking too prime yourself, Tim. I've a square meal a day on the farm, and I'm well looked after with a dry bed of straw in the barn. It's a good life.'

'Will you never go home, Jack?'

Jack's jaw dropped a little, but he seemed to rally when he reminded himself of something. 'I can't now, can I? But I don't mind that so much, really. People go off to America and Canada and places, why shouldn't I stay here, if it's a better life? Sean's cousins went to America, because life got too hard for them in Ireland. We all want a better life, Tim. At home we have two rooms in the house, one up, one down, with the seven of us to sleep and eat there. That's why I joined the army in the first place. Often I had to sleep by the hedge out back, because there was no room in the house. Now I have a prime bed of straw, all to myself, with acres of room - and my own lamp. Mr Robertson is teaching me to read.'

'I'm learning that too,' said Tim, eagerly. 'There's a corporal been told to teach us, like a real schoolroom. We get the Bible mostly, but there's other things too. Like numbers and such.'

Jack nodded. 'Listen,' he said, reaching into his pocket, 'I want you to do something for me, Tim. When you get back to England, as you must one day, please send this letter to my ma, in Norfolk. Mr Robertson helped me write it. It's telling her I'm all right, see. I've told her I'm on a farm here, in the Crimea, but I haven't said which one. You can tell her, if she asks. It's Robertson's farm.'

Tim took the letter, reverently. 'All right, I will, Jack.' He put it inside his jacket pocket. 'I'll tell her you've got a better life. Shall I?'

Jack nodded. 'But don't make it sound as if I think my own home is a shambles. That would upset her. She raised us as best she could. It wasn't her fault we were poor.'

'No, I won't. Good luck, Jack.'

'And to you too, Tim,' said Jack, his face shining in the moonlight. 'I wish you well and happy.'

With that, Jack was gone, into the night like a shadow.

8 ❖ The Bells of Sebastopol

The corporal assigned to teach school was there three half-days of every week. He was in fact supposed to be teaching soldiers, so that they could look after stores and ammunition. It was no good giving a soldier the responsibility of watching over goods unless he had the education to know what was in his charge. But the regiments were wanted on the front line. They were short enough of troops as it was, even though reinforcements were arriving from Britain. Too many soldiers were dying from sickness and living in the open in such harsh conditions.

So the corporal was told to gather up all the spare people around Balaclava, and pass on his reading, writing and numerical skills to them, rather than let them run riot. A regiment minister insisted that if civilian families were taught the Bible they would turn into model citizens and would not take to stealing or other unlawful ways.

In the schoolroom Tim met up with other boys of his own age. 'They're bringing in a siege train,' whispered a youth to Tim one day. 'A steam engine's coming by ship. They're going to lay some tracks and there'll be an engine and some trucks to go on it.'

'Really?'

'Yes – I shouldn't be surprised but we get a ride on it.'

That sounded magnificent. Tim had never seen a railway train. Once school was over, Tim ran all the way back to the hovel, to tell his mother about the steam engine. That night he was so excited he couldn't sleep.

The next day was Sunday. There was a thick mist on the ground right from the earliest light. Tim woke to hear the church and cathedral bells in Sebastopol chiming. They sounded louder and there seemed to be more of them than usual. Perhaps it was a special Sunday in Sebastopol.

Not long after the bells had sounded, the guns began booming along from the front. Tim, Kate and the other women at the hospital were some of the first to find out why. A young soldier turned up there with his wounded friend on his back after carrying him for miles along a muddy road. The wounded soldier was unconscious, but his friend, exhausted from the trip, told everyone what had happened. 'The church bells were the signal to attack. The Russians are pouring over the Inkerman heights. There's a terrible battle going on out there. And the mist is so thick you can hardly see to fight.'

Tim heard this and without telling his mother he began to run along the track from Balaclava to Inkerman. But he soon got tired, for the ground was so boggy he sank to his ankles with every step. By the time he reached Inkerman it was midday. The scene was one of chaos. Fighting had been going on for several hours now and bodies were strewn all over the battlefield. Tim saw Sean on tea-making duty for the regiment and ran over to ask who was winning the battle.

'I don't know, I'm sure,' said Sean. 'There's some terrible fights going on out there. The Guards have lost a deal of men. Some of 'em had to fight with their bare hands, for their cartridges was wet and the rifles wouldn't fire the bullets.'

'Have you seen my dad?'

'Sure, I saw him earlier, Tim, but not since then.'

Tim saw some British officers coming and going on the battleground in brown shooting-suits and carrying walking sticks. Others were in a state of undress. Men had been caught in whatever they were wearing at the time, thinking it was Sunday and no Christian army would attack on such a day. The mists were clearing now and Tim could see small bands of British and French soldiers, some led by officers, others without leaders of rank, were fighting desperate pitched battles against the Russians in ravines and by outcrops of rock. Cannons were firing back and forth, shells whizzing down amongst the combatants. There seemed to be no organisation on either side, simply a frenzied fight to own a small patch of ground or a hill or even just a batch of sandbags piled up to form a wall.

When the fighting was over, British soldiers staggered back to their camps and trenches, dazed and exhausted. They had been outnumbered four to one. Tim heard that ten thousand Russians had fallen, and just two thousand British. The wounds suffered were ghastly. It was by far the worst battle of the war to date. But the Russian attack had been foiled. Once again the allied army had fought off superior odds.

As the day wore on, Tim went from one 95th soldier to the next, asking about his father. Those who didn't know where he was, said so. Others simply avoided his question, saying he should get back to his mother, who would be worried about him. Eventually, Tim did just that. He walked the few miles over the ridge to Balaclava. There he found his mother in a terrible state.

'Oh, Tim,' she cried, taking him into her arms. 'It's your dad. He's been killed, Tim. Your dad's been killed.'

Tim was so stunned by her words his breath left his body and he felt as if he would never breathe again. Eventually, he did suck in air, to follow with a cry, 'Not my dad? Oh, Ma, not my dad! What are we to do? What are we to do?'

She held him, hugging him close, rocking him like a baby, trying to comfort both of them.

'I don't know, son. It's a black day for us. I've seen it happen to others and now it's our turn. It's the lot of a soldier's wife, to lose her husband. Oh, why did I marry a soldier?'

As if grieving for a father and husband wasn't hard enough, Tim and his mother had real practical worries. They were now penniless. There would be no army pay coming to them. There was no one to look after them so far from home. Kate feared they might starve.

But eventually a time did come when they had cried themselves dry, and then Tim said, 'What about Dad's best man, Ma?'

9 ❖ A Wedding

Private Edward Swails was a good, true man. Good as his word to Tim's mother. True to his word to his friend. When he took on the duty of best man at his friend's wedding it meant he was saying, 'If anything happens to you, then I'll marry Kate, so that she and her son won't be stranded thousands of miles from England, with no money.'

Edward came over to see Kate two weeks after the battle. It was the first moment he could get free from his duties. The following week he got permission from his colonel to marry Kate. With a few friends and other soldiers' wives around them they made their vows. Then a broom was laid on the ground and the pair of them held hands and jumped the handle together. No priest was necessary, no registrar. They were married in the eyes of God and that was all poor people like them could ask for.

Witnesses were there, and a new best man had been chosen by Edward. He was seventeen-year-old Peter Sands. He gave his solemn word that should anything happen to Edward, he would take care of Kate and her son. Peter was a bachelor of course. Nothing else would do for the best man at a soldier's wedding, even if it meant that he was much younger than the bride. The marriage was quick, but not hasty. Tim had loved his father, but he also understood that if no one had been prepared to marry his mother, poverty might eat them up as a shark eats its prey. Now they had Edward's pay to support them.

One thing had worried Kate. 'I hear you are a drinking man, Edward?'

'I have been, Kate, but I'm a family man now,' he told her. 'Twice I've been tied to the wheel and flogged for drunkenness. No more of that for me, though. Not with a wife who needs a sober husband, and a boy who needs a father to look up to. I'm a reformed man.'

Kate had to hope this was true, though soldiers often slipped back into their drinking ways, when hard times came. For the time being she had a satisfactory new marriage.

After the Battle of Inkerman a harsh, cruel Russian winter set in. The muddy ground turned to iron furrows. Soldiers stood like statues on sentry duty, frozen to the spot. Ice became the new enemy. The world was numb. Skies turned to marble slabs.

Tim and his mother were taken in by the nurse who ran the little hospital, Mary Seacole, so at least they were well sheltered. Tim woke in the middle of one November night to hear a wind raging outside. 'Ma, what's going on?' he cried, shouting above the noise, as objects crashed into the side of the house. 'It's just a storm,' assured Kate. 'We're all right in here. The walls are nearly a metre thick. But those poor soldiers on the line...'

Tim knew what she meant. There would be no tents out there in such a wind. They would be ripped from their guys and sent flapping like ghosts up into the night. If the force of the wind was tearing benches up and flinging them at the house, then God help the soldiers who had no walls to protect them.

All night long the wind screamed and shrieked in the hollows of the house, as if it were desperate to get in. It shook the door until it rattled on its hinges. It tore shutters from the windows and skimmed them away like playing cards. A flagpole on the roof of another house snapped and hurtled through the open window into Tim's bedroom like a javelin. It buried itself in the inside wall, just above Tim's bed. It was as if the wind were a live, angry creature, bent on chasing Tim and the other camp followers home to Britain and France.

Looking outside, Tim cried, 'Ma, there's chickens being carried off!'

Animals were being swept up, coops and kennels and all. The world was being shaken up. Despite the strong house, Tim was scared for most of the night. The skies had gone mad. Terrified horses in the stables whinnied and kicked at their stalls. Dogs howled. There was pandemonium in the camps.

The following morning was a scene of devastation.

Sean was there, helping to clear the mess from around the village.

'Is it bad in the trenches, Sean?' asked Tim. 'What's the news from the front?'

'You never saw anything like it,' replied Sean. 'I've lost my drum. It rolled and jumped and leaped and almost flew across the ground towards the Russkis. Bang, bang, bang. Bounce, bounce, bounce. I tried to run after it, but the pickets stopped me. They said I would be killed out there in no-man's-land. The Russians have captured my drum, now. I've nothing to rat-a-tat-tat. Look at my fingers twitching! I've only my sticks to play on tin mugs and boxes and nothing else.'

Tim could see that the loss of the drum had upset Sean a great deal. He said, 'It's a prisoner of the enemy now.'

'That it is,' said Sean, 'and I hope they treat it right.'

'They'll give you another drum, Sean. Surely they will?'

'If there's one to give,' snorted the eleven-year-old. 'Sure all the ships sank last night, and everything in them.'

When Tim went down to Balaclava harbour later that day, he saw it was true. Even securely moored ships had been smashed against each other. They were a wreck of tangled and broken masts. There were holes in sides, bows and sterns. Many ships had sunk and all that could be seen were the tips of their masts, sticking out of the water. Tim heard that ships at sea had been lost with many hands. One of them, a supply ship called the *Prince,* had gone down full of precious stores of tens of thousands of boots and clothes. Not only had hundreds of sailors drowned in the seething waters, but the thousands of soldiers waiting for overcoats would freeze to death on the line in the time it took to send for more.

10 ❖ A Flogging Offence

The winter weather got worse. Some fur coats arrived in December but not enough to clothe the whole army. Soldiers were bargaining with local Tartars, buying clothes for themselves. Gone now was the smart look of a clean-shaven, polished-boot, uniformed army. Replaced by a rag-tag army with beards down to their chests. The soldiers had greasy long hair, boots made of bound rags, and a variety of stinking goatskin cloaks and coats to keep them warm. They looked like a mob of barbarians just come down from a long spell in the hills.

Still the guns pounded away at each other and there were small skirmishes in remote spots. Otherwise the two armies stood off from one another.

One day in January, Tim was leaving the schoolroom. There had been no heating in the room and his breath was coming out in sprigs of steam. He just happened to bump into a cavalry officer who was passing by the doorway. Tim sent him flying, sword rattling, spurs jingling. He was a dreadfully smart lieutenant. Tim could see his face in the shine on the lieutenant's boots.

'Watch what you're doing, you little brat!' snapped the lieutenant. 'Damned urchins. Ought to be on a leash.'

The lieutenant was one of the aristocratic officers who had transported trunks full of clothes to Crimea. They had brought silver shaving kits, crates of wine and other luxuries. Some slept in wooden huts or caravans which they had specially built for them. There were servants with them. This officer had a friend with him, who looked sympathetically at Tim.

'The boy didn't mean any harm,' said the lieutenant's friend, who was from a lower rank.

'Mind your own damn business,' said the lieutenant. Then he saw something which he thought had fallen out of his pocket. He picked it up. It was a folded page. He opened it and scanned it. Tim started to walk away. Suddenly the lieutenant called him back.

'Boy! Is this yours?'

Tim looked at the piece of paper which the officer waved, holding it between his thumb and forefinger.

'Yes, sir, please may I have it back?'

Tim reached for it but the lieutenant whisked it out of his reach. Instead, he grasped Tim firmly by the collar and dragged him along with him. The friend protested, but the lieutenant again told him to mind his own business. When the friend began to get angry the lieutenant waved the piece of paper. 'Letter,' he said, abruptly. 'Letter from a deserter.'

Tim's stepfather was sent for. Edward Swails said he knew nothing about the letter. Tim was then hauled up in front of the colonel of the regiment.

Colonel Davis was a stern man with a large nose. He sat on the other side of a table covered in papers. For a while his fingers restlessly wandered through the papers, not really sorting them out, just moving them around. He picked one up and began to read it. Finally, looking down his long nose at Tim, he started to ask some questions.

'Where did you get this letter?'

'My friend gave it to me.'

'Why did he give it to you?'

'So that his ma would know where he is.'

The colonel leaned forward over the table, his eyes small and as hard-looking as flints.

'And where would that be, Timothy?'

Tim saw that he had been trapped.

'I - I don't know. I can't tell you.'

Leaning back into his creaking chair, the colonel laced his fingers together and stared at Tim thoughtfully.

'You realise, Timothy Baker, that I could have you severely punished for assisting a deserter? Flogged? Do you want to be flogged, boy? I can tell you, it hurts.'

'No, sir,' said Tim, the tears springing to his eyes. 'I don't want to be beaten.'

'Then you must tell us where Private John Piggot is hiding.'

For a moment, Tim was thrown, but then he remembered that Jack's real name was John. Jack was his nickname.

'I don't know where he is, sir. He came to me in the night and just gave me the letter. Then he went off again. I don't know where he went. Maybe he's left, sir?'

A thought suddenly occurred to Tim. 'Maybe he went to America?'

The colonel blinked in disbelief. 'America? Why - *how* - would he get to America? Talk sense, Timothy. Desertion in war is a very serious offence.'

'I know, sir,' said Tim, miserably. 'He'll be hanged, or shot, won't he?'

'That's for the Court Martial to decide. Now, I need you to tell me where he is, or it'll be the worse for you too. Do you understand? We're not playing games here.'

Tim began clutching at straws. 'I'm not in the army,' he yelled. 'I'm not a soldier. You can't do things to me.'

'As a family of the regiment, here at the courtesy of the regiment, you are under martial law, boy. Don't make me get angry with you. We need to find Private Piggot. I want that information out of you. I know you're lying. You know where he's gone. You must tell us.'

But Tim refused to reveal the whereabouts of his friend. The colonel sent for his mother, who pleaded with him. His stepfather tried persuasion, then threats. Still Tim would not tell them. Finally the colonel said, 'Throw him in the stockade for the night. Perhaps that'll loosen his tongue.' Kate protested, but the colonel was adamant. 'We must teach him some discipline. If he was one of my drummer boys he'd have been flogged by now. We'll get it out of him. You mark my words.'

11 ❖ Doctor Barry

Tim spent the night in the cells with two drunks and a soldier who had shot one of his own officers and was due to hang in the morning.

Tim kept his eye on the condemned man, terrified of him.

Seeing he was being watched, the man cried, 'Don't judge me! You don't know what he did to me.'

'No, sir,' whispered Tim, 'I won't.'

The man who was to be executed paced up and down all night, muttering to himself in an angry tone. He spoke of murder and mayhem. Tim remained in a constant state of terror.

At first the two drunks fought each other, punching and kicking, but after a while they fell asleep on the dirt floor.

Outside were two sentries who like the condemned man paced up and down, but theirs was an attempt to keep warm, for they kept stamping their boots on the hard ground, and banging their arms around their chests.

In the morning, Tim was let out. They gave him a breakfast of cold porridge, then took him in front of the colonel again.

'Well, boy, have you mended your ways?'

'I can't tell you what I don't know, sir,' said Tim, stubbornly. 'That's all there is to it. You can put me in jail every night, it still won't change things.'

'In that case we'll have to consider putting you on trial.'

Tim's heart began beating very fast. What could they do to him? Could they really flog him? He had seen soldiers being flogged. They were flayed until the blood ran down their backs. Tim's throat became clogged with fear. He didn't want to be whipped. He didn't want to go back into that horrible dark cell with no windows. The colonel was glaring at him, his bushy eyebrows bristling. Tim knew he had to confess now, tell them he knew where Jack was hiding. But his throat was so dry with terror he couldn't get the words out.

There was another man standing in the shadows of the room. This man stepped forward now. A civilian? Tall and thin, he stared down with a kindly face at Tim. His pocket-watch chain dangled as he leaned forward to speak. It glinted in the light shafting through a dirty window.

'The boy seems to have suffered. What's your name?' he asked, in a pleasant voice. 'How old are you?'

'Timothy, sir,' said Tim. 'I'm eleven.'

The man turned to face the colonel who was looking at him with a sour expression.

'Colonel? What's the child done?'

'Refuses to tell me where a deserter is hiding. This doesn't concern you, Dr Barry. You're here to treat my sore throat.'

'Sore throats, or no, colonel, you can't try this child for a criminal offence. The minimum age at which a person in England can be tried for a crime was raised to sixteen, just five years ago. It was held at fourteen for a good few years before that. Where have you been, colonel?'

'India. And this is an army at war in the Crimea, doctor.'

'Nevertheless, if you insist upon this course, I shall become very involved, colonel. I think you are overstepping your authority here. Continue in this and I shall have to raise the matter with Lord Raglan. You ought also to consider Mr Russell, the Irish war correspondent for *The Times*. If he gets wind of such treatment he'll make a pretty story of out it. You know that Queen Victoria never misses a copy of *The Times*. She is particularly keen on knowing what is happening to her soldiers in the Crimea.'

The colonel looked particularly shaken at the mention of Marshal Raglan's name. 'If you're going to throw the queen herself in my face, you'd better take the boy now,' he muttered, going very red.

The man turned to face Tim. 'My name is Dr James Barry,' he said. 'I know the Commander-in-Chief, Lord Raglan, personally. Now, where are you living at this present moment?'

'With my ma,' said Tim, 'outside Balaclava. We used to live in a room with three soldier's wives, but Mother Seacole took us in.'

Mother Seacole, the doctor knew, was a Jamaican woman who had opened a sort of hospital which she called her 'hotel'. Mary Seacole's father had been a British officer and Mary had travelled to England to ask Florence Nightingale if she could be one of her nurses. Miss Nightingale had refused to take her, so Mary made her way to the Crimea at her own expense, and was now treating sick and wounded soldiers.

'I know Mrs Seacole very well,' said Dr Barry. 'I want you to go back to your mother and I'll come this evening.'

'Yes, sir.'

Tim scampered out of the colonel's room as fast as his thin legs would carry him. That evening Dr Barry came to see his mother. Dr Barry explained that it would be better for Tim to leave the Crimea and go back to England.

'While the army thinks Timothy is in possession of the whereabouts of a deserter, they will not leave him alone,' said Dr Barry. 'I know. I'm a military surgeon. I'm familiar with officers like Colonel Davis. He's like a mongrel with a bone. He won't let it go at this. Better to have Tim out of his way and then no harm can come of it.'

'But how will I get him home?' asked Kate, worried.

'I'm on my way back myself,' said Dr Barry. 'I'll take him with me. I sail on the *Redoubt* in two days time. Tim can come with me. Do you have family?'

'My mother, Tim's grandmother, in Derbyshire.'

'Good. I'll see he's safely delivered to her. If you could let me have the address?'

Later, Kate went to speak with her son. 'How do you feel about going back to England, Tim?'

'I'd like it fine. I've had enough of war. It's a dirty business, Ma, and I don't want to be a soldier any more.'

His mother smiled and ruffled his dirty hair.

'Well, I'm glad of that.' She looked at her hand to see something crawling over the back of it. 'I see you've got the lice back. We'll have to wash your hair in some of that herb which Mother Seacole gave us. That'll get rid of them. Now, you get to bed. You've a long journey ahead of you. You know how you like boats. Off you go - and give your mother a kiss before you do.'

Tim kissed his mother's cheek, something he was not over fond of doing now he was a man of close to twelve years, but this was a special occasion. He crawled beneath the thin blankets and tried to forget the cold. England! It seemed a warm memory to him at the moment. Was he ever cold in England? He supposed he must have been, for he remembered snow and ice there too. He tried to recall what his grandmother in Derbyshire looked like and could only remember a face like a creased map and white hair dropping down to thin, bony shoulders.

'It'll be a change,' he told himself, 'if nothing else. And at least Jack will be all right. They won't catch him now, I hope.'

12 ◈ Farewell

The *Redoubt* was due to leave on the next tide. Tim said goodbye to all his friends. He had to go up to the front to see Sean. The fighting was still in progress. By day the British and French guns blasted the defences of Sebastopol, by night the Russians built them up again. It seemed a never-ending cycle.

'Goodbye, Sean. I don't suppose I'll see you again.'

The eleven-year-old Irish boy with old eyes shook Tim's hand gravely. 'You never know, Tim. It's your grandmother's you're going to? Sure, I may come by your way some time with the regiment.'

'I see you've got a new drum.'

Sean grinned and looked at the shiny instrument at his feet, giving it a tap with his toe. 'Got it yesterday. It plays fine, even in this cold weather. It's got a good skin. You can tell.'

Tim left his friend making tea for his company in the shelter of a gun emplacement. When Tim arrived back at Mrs Seacole's 'British Hotel' he found that Dr Barry had gone on ahead of him.

Two 'walking wounded' soldiers from the 95th Regiment were waiting to escort him to the ship. One was Colour Sergeant MacDonald, who had lost his right hand. The other was Private Stillman, whose shoulder blade had been shattered. They were being sent back to Britain to recover from their wounds.

'Let's go, laddie,' said Sergeant MacDonald to Tim. 'Say farewell to yer mother.'

There was a tearful parting which made Tim shrivel inside, but there wasn't time to linger.

The three strolled down to the harbour. People and wagons were coming and going from the port and one or two waved to Tim, knowing he was on his way home. There was envy in some of the eyes. A stiff frost had turned the world white and the hard, rutted ground was slippery and dangerous for the injured men. Soon Tim was about twenty metres ahead, while the two soldiers were deep in some conversation about their wives and families waiting for them back home. As Tim jumped and skipped along the rough track a figure stepped out from behind a hut and seemed to be heading directly for him.

There was something familiar about the person, who was about Tim's size. He was dressed in the heavy fur coat and fur hat that Tartars of the region wore. His face was concealed by the upturned collar and the hat. Closer and closer he came, with the two soldiers still several paces behind. Then Tim recognised the bow legs.

'Oh, Lord,' he muttered.

It was definitely Jack Piggot.

Tim crossed the track to the far side, hoping Jack would keep on walking, his face turned away from the soldiers. Although they were from the same battalion as Jack, the sergeant and private were in a different company. There were eight companies in a battalion. It was possible that they would not recognise Jack. Yet again, they might. Tim knew that the sergeant would definitely arrest Jack on sight. As a senior N.C.O. the sergeant was a responsible man. It was his duty to arrest deserters. Tim knew there was no question of him turning a blind eye.

Yet Jack did not keep on walking! He crossed the track to Tim. When he reached him, he spoke.

'Tim, Mr Robertson heard tell you was arrested by the colonel and was to be flogged. I've come to give myself up. I can't see you beaten for not telling them where I am. It wouldn't be right.'

Tim's heart was beating fast. He glanced behind him. The two soldiers were still deep in conversation. Private Stillman was rubbing his shoulder, which was obviously hurting him.

'Go away!' hissed Tim. 'They're not going to flog me. I'm being sent home.'

Jack looked surprised. 'Those two are not taking you for punishment?'

'Jack – I just said...'

By now the two soldiers were about five paces away.

Tim suddenly shouted, pushing Jack in the chest.

'No, I've no money. Go and beg from someone else, you Tartar!'

Understanding lit up in Jack's eyes. He realised what Tim was doing and stumbled back, dipping his head into his coat. The two soldiers stopped and stared.

Sergeant MacDonald said, 'What's the trouble, Tim?'

'These beggars!' said Tim, in mock anger, as Jack scurried away along the track, a small, hunched, anonymous figure completely wrapped in furs.

'Can't they see we're just as poor as them?'

The sergeant stared at the back of the retreating

figure. For a moment he simply looked, hard. Then he turned back to Tim.

'Laddie, ye cannae blame them. It's this bad winter. We look like rich people alongside some o' the Tartars, ye ken. Why, I feel sorry for some of them.'

Jack was now a small, dark figure heading up into the highlands. At the last moment he turned and gave Tim a wave, before disappearing over the brow of a hill. Sergeant MacDonald was looking away, but Private Stillman noticed the gesture.

'What was that? Did he just signal?'

The sergeant looked up, but Jack was now gone, and he could see nothing.

'Who?'

'That Tartar,' replied Stillman. 'I think he made a rude gesture at our Tim, here. I don't think he likes you, Tim.'

'No,' said Tim, trying hard not to smile, 'I don't suppose he does.'

The three then continued their walk towards the ships in the harbour. Tim thought about his friends Sean and Jack. He hoped the first would survive the war, and the second, homesickness. They both would have time to find their niche. As for Tim himself, he was glad to be going home, glad to be out of the sound of cannons. England was not romantic, and life there was often hard, but it was – home.

THE CRIMEAN PENINSULA

C R I M E A

Eupatoria

Calamita Bay

Simferopol

River Alma

Inkerman Heights

Sebastopol

Yalta

Balaclava

Black Sea

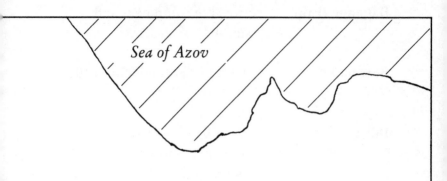

TIM'S JOURNEY

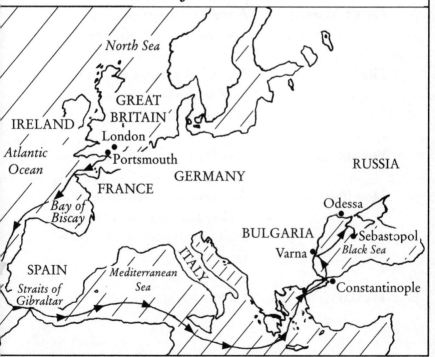

Glossary

Baggage train   movable equipment and supplies of an army

Battalion   A unit of around 800 to 1000 soldiers

Billet   A civilian house where soldiers are lodged temporarily

Cossacks   Russian cavalry regiments

Court Martial   A military court presided over by military officers

Fife   A kind of small, shrill flute used with the drum in military bands

Forage cap   A soldier's peaked cap

Howitzer   A short-barrelled squat-looking gun for firing shells high into the air so that they burst overhead

Hussars   Light cavalry

Kettle	A container for cooking or serving food
Mary Seacole	A Jamaican woman who was turned down by Florence Nightingale when she volunteered to go with Miss Nightingale and her nurses to Scutari Hospital in Constantinople (now Istanbul). She used her own money to get to the Crimea and open up a hospital for the soldiers right next to the battle ground
N.C.O.	Non-commissioned Officer (Lance-Corporal, Corporal, Sergeant, Sergeant-Major)
Pelisse	A fur-lined cloak, part of a soldier's uniform
Picket	A soldier or small group of troops sent out to watch for the enemy
Pipe-clay	Used to whiten a soldier's white straps
Redoubts	A temporary fortification

Rickets	A disease that affects children, caused by vitamin D deficiency, which causes bow legs
Shako hat	British infantryman's tall cylindrical hat, usually with a plume
Sharpshooters	These days they are called marksmen; soldiers who are exceptionally good shots
Shells	Exploding cannonballs, as opposed to **round shot,** which were solid cannonballs
Stoppages	Money 'stopped' or withheld from a soldier's pay for meals, laundry, hair-cutting and cleaning materials
Tartars	Usually called **Tatars** these days, they were the local people who lived in the Crimean region
Zouave	A regiment of a French light infantry corps